SAM SILVER: UNDERCOVER PIRATE

THE DEADLY TRAP

Collect all the Sam Silver: Undercover Pirate *books*

❑ Skeleton Island

❑ The Ghost Ship

❑ Kidnapped

☑ The Deadly Trap

THE
DEADLY TRAP

Jan Burchett and Sara Vogler

Illustrated by Leo Hartas

Orion
Children's Books

First published in Great Britain in 2013
by Orion Children's Books
a division of the Orion Publishing Group Ltd
Orion House
5 Upper St Martin's Lane
London WC2H 9EA
An Hachette UK company

I 3 5 7 9 10 8 6 4 2

Text copyright © Jan Burchett and Sara Vogler 2013
Map and interior illustrations copyright © Leo Hartas 2013

The right of Jan Burchett and Sara Vogler to be identified
as the authors of this work, and the right of Leo Hartas to be
identified as the illustrator of this work have been asserted.

The Orion Publishing Group's policy is to use papers that are
natural, renewable and recyclable products and made from wood grown
in sustainable forests. The logging and manufacturing processes are expected
to conform to the environmental regulations of the country of origin.

A catalogue record for this book is available from the British Library.

ISBN 978 I 4440 0587 5

Printed in Great Britain by Clays Ltd, St Ives plc

For Sally May,
without whom we wouldn't be
where we are today!

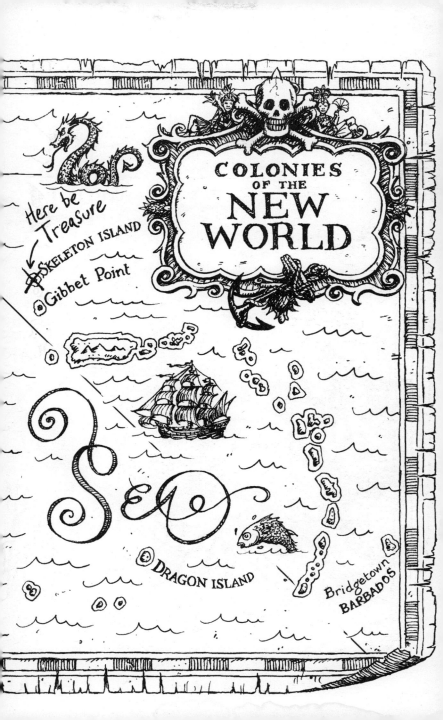

The
SEA
WOLF

Captain's
Cabin
Hammocks
Gun Deck
Galley
Ship's Stores

CHAPTER ONE

"Take that, you villain!" yelled Sam Silver, stabbing viciously at his reflection with a ruler.

He fought his imaginary enemy over his duvet and round a chair and trapped him in the wardrobe. His super sword skill had saved the day! But then, he'd had lessons from experts — a bunch of fierce Caribbean pirates.

It sounded impossible. His home in Backwater Bay was thousands of miles from the Caribbean, and the pirate crew of the *Sea Wolf* had lived three hundred years ago. But Sam had an amazing magic coin to take him there whenever he wanted.

Sam had never forgotten the day he'd found the gold doubloon in a bottle washed up on the beach. It had been sent to him by a pirate ancestor of his, Joseph Silver. When he spat on it and rubbed it, it whisked him back in time to the *Sea Wolf* and its crew of brave buccaneers. The coin was his most prized possession and he kept it in its bottle on a shelf in his bedroom.

Sam swished his ruler wildly in the air, knocking the bottle flying. It hit the lampshade, bounced off his pillow and landed on the floor at his feet. He snatched it up and checked for cracks.

No, it seemed to be OK, but the cork was missing and the coin that should have been inside had gone.

"Disaster!" he cried, scrabbling about on the floor, searching for the precious doubloon.

There was no sign of it. Shining his torch under the bed, he could see something glinting near the wall. He fished it out with a coat hanger. It was only a lump of silver foil. He feverishly searched his bin in case the coin had fallen into it. He found a sock, two apple cores and a squashed sandwich, but no gold doubloon. This was serious. The magic coin seemed to have vanished into thin air! Without it Sam couldn't travel back to the *Sea Wolf*. He gulped at the idea of never seeing his friends, Charlie and Fernando, and the pirate crew ever again.

"Sam!" His mum was calling from their fish and chip shop below the flat. "Can you pop to the supermarket for me? We need some milk."

Sam groaned. How could he concentrate on buying milk when he'd lost his magic doubloon? But he knew he'd be in trouble if he didn't go.

He kept glancing round the room as he slipped his left foot into his trainer.

"Ow!" There was something hard in there. He pulled his foot out and tipped the trainer upside down. The doubloon tumbled out onto the carpet!

Sam snatched it up and held it tightly

in his hands. That had been the worst moment of his life. Then he had a dreadful thought. Supposing the coin had lost its power now he'd dropped it. He'd better check it out. Then he'd go to the shops for his mum. That was the great thing about the magic doubloon. However long his pirate adventure lasted, he knew it would bring him back to exactly the same time in the present – if it still worked.

He pulled on the tatty jeans and T-shirt that he always wore when he went time travelling, and rammed on his trainers. Then he spat on the coin and rubbed it on his sleeve. At once his bedroom whooshed around him in a mad spin. He felt himself being sucked up as if he was in a giant vacuum cleaner.

Sam landed with a thump on the floor of a small wooden storeroom. He could hear the timbers creaking and feel the room swaying. Awesome! He was back on the *Sea Wolf*.

The shouts of the busy crew came from the main deck above. Sam jumped up. His pirate jerkin, belt and neckerchief were on a barrel, along with his spyglass. Charlie always put them there for him. She was the only one who knew he was a time traveller. Everyone else believed he popped home now and then to see his mum, which was true, of course. He just had a longer journey than they realised.

Stowing his coin safely in his jeans pocket, he threw on his pirate clothes and grabbed his spyglass. He ran up the stairway, bursting out onto the bright, sunlit deck. The blue ocean sparkled, the patched sails were tight in the wind and the flag with its snarling wolf's head and crossed bones fluttered merrily at the top of the mast.

Someone had hung some washing on a line strung across the deck. Ragged shirts and breeches flapped in the breeze.

I didn't know pirates had washday! thought Sam. *Hope I don't have to do the ironing!* He ducked under the line of clothes to find the crew and cannoned straight into someone coming the other way.

"Sorry," he gasped. "I was—" He stopped. He was looking up into a face he'd never seen before. What had happened? He was on the right ship, but where was the *Sea Wolf* crew?

CHAPTER TWO

For a moment the man looked astonished. Then he gave a deep laugh. "Where did you spring from, young'un. A stowaway, are you?" He gave Sam a friendly punch on the arm. "Have you been hiding in the hold?"

The man was tall and broad, with crinkly, smiling eyes. He seemed friendly enough but what was he doing here? Sam felt a dull ache in his stomach. Where were all his shipmates and Crow, his parrot friend? Was the coin damaged after all? Had it brought him back to the right ship but the wrong time?

"Sam!" came a cry. Sam knew that voice. A grin of relief spread over his face as Charlie, with her ragged hair and boy's shirt and breeches, rushed up beside him.

"I'm glad you're back!" she said, sliding her arm through his.

"And I'm glad to see you!" Sam burst out. "I didn't spot anyone I knew at first and I thought the coin must have brought me back to a different— Ouch!"

Charlie had stepped firmly on his toe. "This is Sam Silver," she said to the man. "We told you about him. He comes to join us when his mum doesn't need him, don't you Sam? And he never knows how long it will take him to get here."

"Er, that's right," agreed Sam, rubbing his foot. He could always rely on Charlie to get him out of trouble. It would have been a disaster to talk about time travel to this man. He'd think Sam was possessed by an evil demon.

"So you're Sam Silver," said the man, beaming as he shook Sam's hand. "I'm Dick Gudgeon. I've only been on this ship for two weeks but I've heard all about you. Pleased to make your acquaintance. The captain thinks very highly of you, you know."

Sam felt his face turning red with the praise.

"But you came aboard without anyone seeing!" Dick went on, looking keenly at him. "You're a clever lad to do that. Where does your mum live?"

"That's Sam's

business," said Charlie quickly. "He doesn't tell us and we don't ask."

"And that's all right with us!" came a deep voice. Captain Blade strode up, the weapons in his belts gleaming in the sun. "Glad to have you back," he told Sam. "I see you've met our new crew member. He came aboard in Tortuga when we stopped for supplies. Dick's been a doing a good job of lookout while you've been gone."

"Just doing my duty," said Dick modestly.

"Does that mean you won't need me up in the crow's nest, Captain?" asked Sam, disappointed. He loved being lookout boy, watching the seas from the wooden basket at the top of the mainmast with Crow on his shoulder, and warning the crew when he spied an enemy vessel. He could see a flash of green feathers, which meant the parrot was up there at this very moment, waiting for him.

"Of course I'll need you, Sam," Blade

told him. "You're a first-rate lookout. Besides, we could do with Dick's help on deck. He's an expert sailor and can turn his hand to anything."

"Shiver me timbers," declared Harry Hopp, his wooden leg thumping on the deck as he came to join them. "Dick's worth his weight in gold."

"He really is," came a Spanish voice from the rigging.

Fernando jumped down next to Sam and slapped him on the back in welcome. Sam noticed that a new earring shone in his ear under his wild curly hair. He'd ruined the last one picking a lock. "You've got here at the right time, my friend," Fernando told him. "Dick's going to lead us to a great hoard of treasure."

"Aye," agreed the new crew member, rubbing his hands. "I heard of a ship, the *Queen Bess*, that's setting sail from Barbados. There's gold on her like you've never seen! Seems a waste to let all that wealth go to England."

"So we wait till she's at sea and ambush her!" cried Sam eagerly.

"Not so fast, lad!" laughed Captain Blade. "She'll be heavily guarded by a fleet of men-o'-war."

"I suggested to your captain that we take her treasure while she's still at anchor in Bridgetown port," said Dick.

Sam felt a thrill of excitement. Then a doubt suddenly popped into his head. "But you must have come from another pirate crew," he said to Dick. "Won't they be after it, too?"

"I like a boy with a quick mind," replied Dick. "No, my last crew were lost in a terrible storm. I was the only survivor . . ." He broke off and Sam saw the sheen of tears in his eyes.

"Aye, but you've got new shipmates now," said Captain Blade gruffly, giving Dick a kindly pat on the shoulder. "Get to your posts, men. We'll be reaching Barbados in a few hours. Sam, you're on lookout."

He turned abruptly and walked straight into a flapping shirt. "And someone get this washing off my deck!"

Dick Gudgeon was smiling again now. "This is a fine ship," he said. He looked Sam up and down. "And you've got the makings of a fine pirate. You're quick-witted and canny. You'll be a captain one day, I'll be bound!"

Sam glowed with pride as he climbed the rigging towards the crow's nest. This adventure might be the best yet!

CHAPTER THREE

That afternoon Sam sat with Dick on the foredeck. Dick was teaching him some new knots. The north coast of Barbados had been sighted an hour ago and now they were heading south for Bridgetown. Sam felt the excitement bubbling up and he had to fight to keep his hands steady. Not only did this treasure sound awesome, but they were going to sneak in and take it from under the noses of the authorities. It was like being in an adventure film.

While Sam practised his clove hitch knot, Dick whistled an old tune, *Greensleeves*, and made a loop on the end of a piece of rope. Sam stopped and watched in amazement. His new shipmate had enormous hands, but he worked the ropes together as if he were stitching the finest embroidery.

"That must have taken you a long time to learn," said Sam.

"Not if you've lived all your life on a ship, my lad," said Dick genially. "I could easily teach a clever boy like you to splice rope as well as I do." He picked up a wooden stick and pushed the sharp end through the rope. "See, I take my fid to make the hole and then—"

"Swab the decks!" came a hoarse cry and the ship's parrot flapped down to perch on Sam's shoulder.

"Hello there, Crow," said Dick, stroking his head. "He's kept me good company when I've been on lookout." He dug about in the pockets of his breeches. "I've got some maize seed somewhere." He pulled out a handful of yellow seeds and held them out. Crow gave a delighted squawk and tucked in. "They love sunflower seeds too, but you mustn't give him too many — they'll make him fat!"

"You know a lot about parrots," said Sam, impressed.

"I had one when I was a boy," Dick told him. "Beautiful bird. I called him Drake."

"Drake!" squawked Crow.

"What a fantastic pirate name!" laughed Sam. "We call this one Crow to keep the captain happy."

Dick looked confused. "Why would that make Captain Blade happy?"

"Because that way he can pretend Crow is a real crow," explained Sam. "Of course, he doesn't really think that, but it's the only way he'll allow Crow on board. He's scared of parrots, you see."

"Scared of parrots!" exclaimed Dick, dropping his rope. "I thought Blade was fearless. I did wonder that he never went near the bird."

He fell silent and Sam felt terrible. Everyone else on board knew about Captain Blade's one fear and it didn't bother them. But Dick was a new member of the crew. He might be disappointed in the captain of the *Sea Wolf* and decide not to stay. And that meant they wouldn't get the gold in Bridgetown.

Dick Gudgeon had a curious expression on his face. To Sam's surprise it wasn't disappointment. He was grinning! Dick seemed to find the captain's fear funny. But it wasn't a nice grin. It was a grin that sent a chill through Sam.

Dick saw Sam staring and the expression was gone in an instant. "Well, well," he said, shaking his head sympathetically. "Each of us has his faults. Blade's still a fine, brave man, for all that."

"The bravest!" declared Sam. "He'll outfight anyone who threatens the *Sea Wolf* and its men."

"I've no doubt of it," replied Dick thoughtfully. He stood up. "You've learned those knots mighty quick, Sam.

I'll be off to help the bosun with the new fore rail."

Sam watched him go in search of Ned. Dick Gudgeon was a great shipmate. He was a hard worker and everyone liked him. But something niggled inside Sam's brain: why had he looked pleased to hear of the captain's fear?

With Crow clinging tightly to his jerkin, Sam went to find Charlie. He'd tell her what he'd seen. She'd know what to do.

Charlie was sitting on the poop deck with a fishing rod, the line dangling over the side. Sinbad, the ship's cat, lay curled at her feet. Crow took one look, gave a squawk and flew up to the top of the mast. The cat watched him go then began to wash his paws.

"Who's the softest kitty in the world?" said Charlie. Sinbad rolled over and let her tickle his belly.

Sinbad adored Charlie but greeted everyone else with a flash of his claws.

Keeping his distance, Sam told his friend what he'd seen.

"I don't think you've given Dick a fair chance," said Charlie, when he'd finished. "He's helpful and friendly and really useful. Why would he tell us where to find gold if he meant us harm?"

"You're right," sighed Sam. "I can't explain what I saw. I only know that his smile made me go cold."

Charlie put her hand on Sam's forehead. "You haven't got a fever, have you?" she asked with a grin.

"I'm as well as you are," insisted Sam.

"Then I'm sure you were mistaken," said Charlie.

Sam frowned. He liked to think of himself as a cool detective, but he had to admit he did sometimes get a bit overexcited. He remembered reporting a suspicious-looking person in the school playground. It had turned out to be the new vicar who was very surprised when a policeman tried to arrest him. Sam certainly didn't want to make a fool of himself like that. He'd be too ashamed to visit the *Sea Wolf* ever again!

"Maybe I'm imagining things," he admitted, "but I'm going to keep my eye on Dick from now on."

"And so will I," Charlie assured him. "Just in case."

Sam walked across the deck, making for

the rigging. It was his turn up in the crow's nest. As he grasped the knotted rope ready to climb, he spotted Dick and Ned repairing a piece of broken rail. Dick was holding a length of wood as Ned sawed.

"I feel sorry for Captain Blade," Dick was saying. "I mean, I wouldn't like to be scared of parrots. There are so many around these parts."

Sam quickly hid by the galley door and watched.

"It could be worse," Ned answered as he cut into the wood. "We just keep Crow out of his way. I heard it's because one stole his porridge when he was a young 'un." Ned grinned. "We're lucky it's only them he's scared of and not ghosts, or storms — or the enemy!"

"Too right," agreed Dick. "But what happens if a parrot comes near him?"

"He goes as white as my shirt," said Ned. He glanced at his grimy clothes.

"That is, when my shirt was new!"

"Is that all?" laughed Dick. "It doesn't sound like any great fear."

"Not to you or me, I suppose," said Ned. "But the captain's always happier when Crow's not nearby."

"Good job there's only one parrot on board then," said Dick, looking thoughtful.

Sam pulled himself up the rigging and swung himself into the wooden crow's nest at the top. His mind was racing. Why was Dick Gudgeon so interested in the captain's fear of parrots?

"Scurvy sea dog!" squawked Crow, landing on his shoulder.

"You've hit the nail on the head there," Sam told the green parrot. "I reckon Dick's not the man the crew thinks he is."

But he had to prove it. And there was only one way — he'd have to make a plan to catch Dick out!

Chapter Four

Late that afternoon the *Sea Wolf* lay at anchor off the coast of Barbados. The crew were trying to eat a fish stew. At least that's what Peter the cook called it. Sam decided it tasted more like dirty dishwater with the dirty dishes still in it!

"Well, I'll polish the portholes with a piranha!" said Ned, spitting out a bone.

"This treasure will be a fine haul. We can stash it on Skeleton Island."

Sam watched Dick intently, but the new crew member was as cheerful and friendly as ever.

"The *Queen Bess* is carrying a lot of gold," he laughed. "I hope you've got plenty of room for it in that stronghold of yours."

The pirates rubbed their hands at the thought of all the booty.

"You'll be setting foot there yourself," Captain Blade told him. "But you'll understand that we'll need to blindfold you when we get near. We'll let you see where it is when we know you better."

"I wouldn't have it any other way, Captain," said Dick earnestly. "In my book, a man must prove himself worthy and I'll do anything to earn that trust."

"I reckon it won't be long!" called Harry.

"Aye!" chorused the crew enthusiastically.

Sam's brain was buzzing. Dick Gudgeon didn't know where the pirates' stronghold was. He said he was happy to wait until the captain chose to tell him, but was that true? If Dick wasn't the loyal shipmate everyone believed, then Sam was certain he'd want to know where the *Sea Wolf* treasure was stored right now! A plan began to form in his head. He'd make a false map of the location of Skeleton Island and hide it somewhere. Then he'd tell Dick where he'd put it and wait to see what happened.

The crew were astonished at the sight of Sam gulping his stew down and heading off to the galley with his tin plate.

"Surely the boy doesn't want seconds!" he heard Harry Hopp exclaim.

Once he was inside the small ship's kitchen, Sam put his plate down and took a burned stick from the cooking fire. Then he sneaked down to the storeroom. He found an old piece of sail and sketched a quick map of the Caribbean with the blackened end of the stick. He drew a blob of an island right in the middle of the western sea, as far away from Skeleton Island as he could – and put an X on it.

He looked around for a hiding place for his map – somewhere that no one else would discover unless they were told about it. But there seemed to be nowhere really safe. If he put it in a box or barrel someone might open it. As he wandered round the storeroom he caught his foot on a nail that was sticking up. He looked down. One of the floorboards was loose. Sam got his fingers under it and pulled until the wood came away. He pushed his map into the little gap below and placed the board back.

"Now to give Dick the bait," he muttered, "and see if he takes it." He grabbed some rope and went in search of the new crewman. He found him sitting by the bowsprit, carving an intricate pineapple shape into the round end of his wooden fid.

"I'm sorry to bother you," said Sam, holding out the rope, "but I can't remember the clove hitch you showed me. Can you help?"

"Of course," said Dick with a friendly grin. He took the rope, looped and threaded it round the rail, and pulled it tight. "See what I'm doing? It's simple, especially for a bright boy like you."

"I'm not bright," said Sam, looking down as if he was sad. "I'm no good at remembering things. Like that knot — and which side is port and which is starboard. Don't tell anyone, but I only remember the location of our secret hideout because I've made a map."

He studied Dick's face as he spoke, but the man's expression didn't change.

"Well," said Dick, untying the rope. "I hope you've got that map good and hidden. You wouldn't want it to fall into the wrong hands if an enemy boarded the *Sea Wolf*."

"They'd never find it," said Sam eagerly. "It's hidden under a loose plank in the storeroom floor."

Dick nodded. "Good place!"

Sam jumped up. "I'm on lookout in a minute," he said. "Thanks for your help with the knot."

"Happy to oblige, lad," said Dick. "I'll be heading off to my hammock."

Sam left the foredeck, but instead of making for the rigging he dived down the hatchway to the storeroom. He wasn't really on lookout duty.

He just wanted Dick to think he was as far away as possible. He hid behind an empty barrel. If Dick Gudgeon was as honourable as he pretended then he would go straight to bed and not seek out the map. Sam hoped that was exactly what would happen. The crew really liked Dick and it would be awful to disappoint them.

Sam waited. He wondered how long he was going to have to stay squashed behind the barrel. He'd need to come out eventually or the crew would come looking for him, and they'd think he was mad if he said he was playing hide-and-seek.

He was beginning to think he'd been wrong about his new shipmate, when . . .
Creak!

The storeroom door slowly opened. Sam peeped round his barrel. Someone was coming in!

CHAPTER FIVE

A tall figure crept into the storeroom. He was holding a lantern. When he turned Sam could see his face in the flickering candlelight. It was Dick Gudgeon! He carefully closed the door behind him and crept across the floor, testing each board with his foot.

Sam tried to slow his breathing down,

terrified that he could be heard, but Dick was too busy searching. Sam stayed stock still as Dick moved towards the map's hiding place. Suddenly he dived down, placed the lantern beside him and put his fingers round the loose floorboard. In an instant he had the map in his hand. After a furtive look about him, he studied it in the lantern light and let out a low laugh.

Got him! thought Sam. Now to show the crew the truth about Dick Gudgeon.

"You villain!" he yelled, leaping up and sending the barrel rolling. "I knew you weren't to be trusted."

Dick turned on him. There was no sign of the friendly expression he always wore in front of the crew. His face was boiling with fury as he gripped the map in one hand and curled his other fist, ready to strike. "Shut your stupid mouth!" he hissed, aiming a vicious punch at Sam. "Or I'll shut it for you."

Sam dodged the blow. "We'll see what
the captain has to say about this!" He
flung open the storeroom door. "Help!" he
shouted at the top of his voice. "Captain
Blade! Harry! Everyone! Come here
quickly!"

Footsteps thundered and Captain Blade
appeared, cutlass drawn. Harry Hopp and
Fernando were close behind.

"What in blazes is going on here?"
demanded the captain.

"Dick Gudgeon's trying to find out where our hideout is," cried Sam, pointing accusingly at Dick. "He's no friend of the *Sea Wolf*!"

But the evil expression had completely vanished from Dick's face. He held out the piece of sail, smiling pityingly at Sam. "I think the poor lad is talking about this," he said. "He told me he'd made a chart of where your hideout lies."

"Blow me down!" exclaimed Harry Hopp, horrified.

"Don't be hard on him," Gudgeon went on in a pleading voice. "He's a bit simpleminded. I was going to destroy it before it fell into the wrong hands." As he spoke, he crushed the sail up, rubbing it between his palms to obliterate the charcoal drawing.

"That's not true!" yelled Sam. "He wanted to . . ."

He stopped as he realised that everyone

was staring at him. Harry was shaking his head.

"You put down where our stronghold is!" gasped Fernando. "But it's a sacred secret."

"I thought you knew that, Sam," snapped Captain Blade.

"Don't worry on my account," said Dick pleasantly. "I didn't so much as glance at it. I've told you, I don't want to know where it is until the captain thinks I'm worthy." He handed the piece of sail to Blade and left, whistling *Greensleeves* as if he didn't have a care in the world.

"You have to believe me, Captain," gabbled Sam. "I hid the map as a test to see if Dick would fall for it — and he did. But it was a false—"

"Avast your jabbering!" Blade's face looked sharp and stern in the lantern light. "I cannot believe you're accusing an honest man of treachery. Dick Gudgeon has done nothing to deserve that."

"But . . . I . . ." spluttered Sam.

"You're acting very strangely, Sam," said Fernando looking puzzled.

"I'll not have a crew member make trouble on board," roared the captain. "You are never to do that again. Do you understand?"

Sam hung his head. "Yes, sir," he muttered.

"Then we'll say no more about it."

The captain spun on his heel and left with Harry Hopp stomping behind him. Fernando opened his mouth as if to speak, then seemed to change his mind and left without a word. Sam found himself alone.

Charlie slipped in, Sinbad in her arms. The ship's cat stared at Sam as if he was accusing him as well.

Sam flopped miserably down onto the floor. "I suppose you've come to have a go at me too."

But to his surprise Charlie shook her head. "I know you must have had good reasons for accusing Dick," she said, settling down beside him. "But I don't understand. Why did you make a map of Skeleton Island? That was really stupid."

"I was trying to catch Dick out," sighed Sam. He told her about his plan. "And it worked," he finished bitterly, "but no one believes me."

Charlie put her hand on his arm. "*I* believe you," she said solemnly.

Sam gave her a grateful smile. "Dick Gudgeon's a dangerous man to have on board. He's after our gold and I reckon he'll stop at nothing to get it!"

Charlie gave a shiver. "This is serious. Dick's such a good actor that everyone else thinks he's an honest man."

"Then we've got to show them they're wrong," muttered Sam, "before it's too late!"

"I agree," said Charlie, "but we mustn't let Dick know we're working together."

"Then you have to pretend not to be my friend any more," said Sam, "and that's going to be horrible."

CHAPTER SIX

That night Sam lay in his hammock on the gun deck. He felt very lonely all on his own. No one had come near him after the map had been found, although he could tell that Dick Gudgeon was keeping a crafty eye on him and Fernando was throwing him puzzled looks. He realised it must be hard for the crew. Sam only sailed with them now and again. Dick had worked alongside them for two whole weeks, and he'd brought the promise of treasure.

Sam wondered how he was ever going to find evidence that the man was a villain. It wasn't as if he could overhear Dick having a conversation on a mobile, or read one of his emails. He decided it was much harder being a detective three hundred years ago, before those handy things had been invented.

Sam drifted into a dream where he was fighting a shark that had Dick Gudgeon's evil, grinning face. The shark kept coming at him, its teeth sharp and vicious, and no matter how fast he swam, it wouldn't go away.

Suddenly he woke with a start. He could hear a faint scuffling noise. At first he wondered if it was a rat — but he was used to them scurrying about. What was it then? Not someone going to bed, that was

for sure. The pirates always clumped around, throwing belts to the floor with a clatter, and yawning and belching loudly as they clambered into their hammocks. No, this sounded like someone who didn't want to be heard.

Sam cautiously opened one eye. Dick was standing on the other side of the deck. Something told Sam he'd better pretend to be asleep. He lay still and watched. A lantern swung at the far end of the gun deck. By its faint light Sam could see that Dick had laid his sailor's bag on his bed. He was carefully feeling inside it in the gloom. He swung round suddenly as if he knew he was being spied on. Sam shut his eyes just in time. He waited a few seconds until he could hear Dick searching in his bag again. He opened his eyes a sliver to see Dick pull out a long tube wrapped in oilskin. Dick looked furtively about, then made to stash the scroll in his shirt.

But there was a sudden noise above, as if someone was about to come down to the gun deck. Dick hurriedly thrust the roll under his pillow and was gone.

When Sam was sure it was safe to move he crept over to Dick's hammock, his heart thumping hard. He had to know what was so important about that tube. It must be precious to Dick or he wouldn't have been checking it so secretly and hiding it from the crew. Sam plunged his hand under the pillow and retrieved it. His fingers trembled with excitement as he undid the oilskin wrapping to reveal a parchment. He smoothed it out, but he was deep in the shadows and couldn't read any of the words. He crept silently along the deck, hoping none of the crew would choose that moment to come to bed. He stopped under the swinging lantern and read the beautifully written words in front of him.

The bearer of this letter is on secret official business and is to be given safe passage on the island of Barbados.

Bevil Granville, Governor

There was a red wax seal on the bottom, next to the signature.

Sam stared at the letter, his brain working furiously. Dick Gudgeon was on official business for the governor! And Sam knew that every governor of every Caribbean island was an enemy of the pirates.

What was Dick up to? The crew always

said that the authorities were no better than pirates themselves. So why had Dick come to the captain with the information about the gold? A worm of an idea wriggled in his brain. Could it be that the governor of Barbados was paying Dick to steal the gold from the *Queen Bess*? And that Dick had decided to use the *Sea Wolf* crew to do it for him? Then, when they thought they were safely away, the *Sea Wolf* would be captured and the gold would be taken by Dick and Governor Granville.

The pirates would be thrown into prison and Dick could then go to their hideout on Skeleton Island and pinch the booty stored there, too. That would also explain why he wanted to know where the stronghold could be found. But the villain wasn't going to get away with it. Sam looked at the parchment again. Here was the evidence to prove to the captain and crew that Dick was not to be trusted.

He spun round, ready to make for the steps up to the deck — and stopped dead. Dick Gudgeon was standing in his path. He wore a nasty smirk of delight on his face, and he held a knife out in front of him.

"You're not going anywhere," he snarled.

CHAPTER SEVEN

"That's my letter and for my eyes only," hissed Dick Gudgeon. "You're a little thief. And thieves deserve to die!" He lunged at Sam, the point of his dagger aiming straight at his heart.

Sam threw himself to the floor. He scuttled like a crab towards the cutlass store, but Dick had already barred the way.

Sam got to his feet to face him, the parchment gripped tightly in his hand. He mustn't let Gudgeon have it back. The angry man swished his dagger in front of Sam, weaving it skilfully like a cobra about to strike.

"You can't stab me and get away with it," said Sam desperately. He darted behind the nearest hammock. "The captain and the crew would find you standing over my body."

"What body?" said Dick nastily. "There won't be one. I'll dispose of it through a porthole. No one will wonder where you've gone. You're always popping off to see your mother." He lunged again, slashing the canvas bed between them. "And they won't miss you either. They all think you're stupid so they'll be glad to see the back of you."

Sam remembered how the captain and Harry Hopp had looked at him in the storeroom. Dick was probably right. But he wasn't going anywhere while his crew were in danger. He glanced around, but he couldn't see anything to defend himself with, just the mop and bucket for swabbing the deck.

He grabbed the mop and thrust the wet end into Dick's face, earning himself valuable seconds while his attacker tried to untangle himself.

But Sam knew he couldn't hold out for long. He had to get help. He snatched up the bucket and banged it hard against the hull. It gave out a tremendous clang and he yelled at the top of his voice at the same time. Dick launched himself at Sam with a furious roar.

Sam jumped aside and found himself staggering back against a pile of cannonballs. Before Dick could get to him he'd pushed the pile over, sending them thudding loudly on to the deck.

"You crafty little devil!" growled Dick. He caught Sam by the shirt. Sam tried to move but it was no good. Dick's knife was raised to strike.

At that moment there was a clattering of footsteps from the hold below. Dick let out an oath and relaxed his grip. "I'll deal with you later," he spat viciously, "when there's no one around."

Sam sprang to his feet. Even though Gudgeon was now pretending to look innocent, the crew would soon realise the truth when they saw the letter! "He was going to kill me!" he shouted as Fernando ran up to him with Ned and Ben close behind, carrying lanterns.

"What are you rambling about now, Sam Silver?" said Ben. His eyes fell on the cannonballs scattered over the floor. "We thought we heard thunder and it turns out to be you playing bowls with the ammunition!"

"Well, I'll go to Jamaica in a gin jug," declared Ned. "I think he's lost his wits. We must tell the captain."

"Aye," said Dick sorrowfully. "It's the only thing to do."

"You don't understand!" yelled Sam. "Dick's working for the governor of Barbados. I found this letter giving him safe passage."

"I'll have that!" came Captain Blade's stern voice. The captain strode along the length of the gun deck and took the paper with a flourish. As he read it a furious expression came over his face.

"I saw him take it out of his bag," insisted Sam, "and hide it under his pillow."

"Explain yourself, Dick Gudgeon," said the captain fiercely.

Good, thought Sam. *There's no way he can wriggle out of this now!*

"The boy *says* it was in my bag, but you'll notice he's the one holding it," said

Dick, with a wide-eyed expression. "I've never seen it before."

"Liar!" cried Sam. "You only want the *Sea Wolf* to steal the gold from the *Queen Bess* so that you and the governor can share it between you!"

But Dick was staring earnestly at the captain. "I came down to sleep and saw the boy with the paper. I just asked him, friendly-like, if it was a letter from his mother and he turned on me."

"That's not true," gasped Sam. "He attacked *me* with a knife."

Dick held up his hands. They were empty. Sam realised with a sinking heart that somehow he'd got rid of his dagger. "If my name is on that letter," Dick told the captain, "then throw me overboard now."

"There's no name written here," said Blade.

"But it really is his letter," pleaded Sam desperately. The pirates were looking at him as if he was something they'd emptied out of the bilge pump. "It was in his bag," Sam repeated, but the words sounded weak.

"I had the notion that this lad was a bit simple when he put down your stronghold on a map," said Dick, "but now I realise I was wrong. He's not simple at all. He's a nasty piece of work. He did that map to show the governor. And this letter of safe passage on Barbados proves it. He's a spy for Sir Bevil Granville." He looked at the grim faces round him. "And if I were you I'd check you've still got your weapons." He delved under the blanket in Sam's hammock and produced his own knife. "I saw him steal this from my bag."

"But I . . ." protested Sam.

"The foolish boy didn't know I was watching," Dick went on. "He'd have had us all without arms by the time we reached Bridgetown."

"Easy pickings for the governor's men!"

said Fernando. Sam could hear the shock in his voice. Fernando was looking at him as if he couldn't believe the things he was hearing. "What a false friend!" he murmured sadly.

"And happy enough to steal from a fellow crewmate," muttered Ben angrily.

Captain Blade's piercing blue eyes fixed Sam with a look that felt like a stab in the heart. "We'll deal with you later," he snapped. "We'll not delay our treasure plan. Lock Silver up, Ned, where he can't do any more harm."

"No!" Sam's cry echoed around the gun deck. "Please, Captain, you've got to believe me."

But Captain Blade merely folded the letter and shoved it in his pocket. "Everyone to your posts!" he barked as he spun on his heel and headed back up on deck, followed by Ben.

Ned's huge hand grabbed Sam's arm and held him fast. He pushed him towards the stairway.

Fernando looked away as Sam went past.

"I didn't do anything wrong," Sam told his friend desperately. "You believe me, don't you?"

"I wish I could," muttered Fernando. "But everything is telling me that you're a traitor to the crew."

Sam let Ned haul him up the stairs. He had never felt so awful in his life. He twisted back to try and plead with Fernando one last time, but Dick Gudgeon was standing in the way. He shot Sam a look of triumph.

Sam shivered. The man was evil, and he meant the *Sea Wolf* pirates harm. He was sure of it.

CHAPTER EIGHT

Sam shifted about, trying to get comfortable. He was locked in a wooden cage on the foredeck and his bottom had gone numb. The cage had been used for goats and it stank of dung and sour milk. The crew were going about their business, throwing him dirty looks.

Gazing round the lantern-lit deck,

Sam could see Charlie heading for the galley. He called to her in a low voice.

She looked up at him, tossed her head and moved on out of sight. Sam gulped. Was she pretending to hate him or did she believe Dick Gudgeon's story now? If she'd turned against him too then he didn't have a single friend on the *Sea Wolf*. Well, even if he had to act alone, one thing was certain — he was descended from a brave pirate and he wasn't going to give up!

"Bridgetown's just a mile up the coast from here," said a voice. It was Dick. He was walking with the captain across the main deck. They stopped under one of the lanterns.

"The *Sea Wolf* is too recognisable," answered Captain Blade. "We can't just sail into the harbour. We'll be shot out of the water."

"You're right, Captain," said Dick. Sam squirmed as he heard the falseness in the man's tone. "And my information is at least two weeks old. I can't be sure exactly where the *Queen Bess* will be anchored."

Sam peeped through his fingers and saw the captain pulling at the braids in his beard as he considered the matter. "We'll check that before we make our final plan," he said. "She doesn't sail for another day, I believe."

"Then I volunteer to go ashore," said Dick. "While it's still dark, I'll make my way along the coast on foot and see what I can spy in the harbour. There'll be plenty of soldiers about but, with luck,

I might manage to avoid them. Though, of course, it would be easier with two men . . ."

Blade stroked his beard as Dick went on.

"If I get through and report back we can decide how to lighten the *Queen Bess* of her load. If I don't return by the end of the day you'll know it was too risky, but you'll have time to make your escape from these waters. And only one man will have been lost."

Sam watched as the captain grasped Dick's shoulder. He wanted to call out for him not to trust the man, but he had to bite his tongue.

"I agree it's a job for two men," said Blade. "It's too dangerous for you to go alone. I will go with you."

"No, your life is more important to your men and your ship than mine," protested Dick, although Sam thought he saw a small smile playing round his lips in the lantern light. "Of course I would feel invincible with you by my side, but . . ."

Blade held up his hands. "I will hear no argument. It will be safer for two than one."

"Thank you, sir," said Dick humbly. "I'll be glad to have my captain as my companion. I can think of no one better."

"We'll take Fernando with us," said the captain. "He can slip aboard the *Queen Bess* like a cat and not be seen."

"No need," replied Dick quickly. "I can do that. We don't want to put the lad in danger."

Captain Blade nodded and looked up at the dark sky. "We'll leave within the half hour," he said. "That should give us enough of the night for cover. I'm going to give Harry Hopp his instructions before I go."

Sam watched as he strode away to

his cabin, calling to his first mate as he went. Sam felt more helpless than ever. The captain had complete trust in Dick Gudgeon and was going ashore with him. And Sam was certain that that was what Dick had wanted all along, even though he'd *said* he was happy to go alone. What was the man up to?

Dick cast a furtive look around, then took the lantern from its hook. He crept to the rail and lifted it so it was shining

towards the shore. He raised his hand in front of the flame, held it there for a moment and then moved it away. Sam saw him make exactly the same action three more times.

He's giving a signal! he thought with alarm. He stared intently at the coastline, black against the starlit sky.

At that moment there was an answering light from somewhere along the dark shore further down the coast.

Sam was horrified. Dick must have an accomplice. There might even be more than one! And they were sure to be the governor's men. But that didn't make sense. Why would they show up now? If Sam was right and Dick wanted the *Sea Wolf* crew to steal the treasure, then surely the governor's troops wouldn't make an appearance until the booty was on board!

And then the truth hit Sam. Dick had

cleverly made sure that it was the captain who went ashore with him and no one else. It wasn't treasure that the governor and Dick were after – it was Captain Blade himself!

CHAPTER NINE

The door to the captain's cabin opened. Quick as a flash, Dick returned the lantern to its hook.

Blade and Harry Hopp joined him at the rail.

"Captain!" called Sam. "You mustn't go. It's a trap!"

The captain looked at him, his face hard as rock in the lanternlight. "I'll deal with you on my return," he said in a low, chilling voice. "If you take my advice, you'll keep your mouth closed until then. I doubt any of the crew will want to hear from you."

"But I'm telling the truth," pleaded Sam. "Mr Hopp, listen to me. The captain's in great danger."

"Aye, that's what you would want, I'll warrant!" snapped the first mate. "You scurvy snake. The captain's right. Keep your mouth shut or he'll return to find an empty cage and a shark with a full belly!"

Some of the crew came to see the shore party off. Sam spotted Fernando and Charlie among his shipmates at the rail, but they didn't even glance at him.

Splat! Something hit the side of the cage, spraying Sam with a stinking mess of rotten tomato. At last the crew went away, muttering curses under their breath. Sam saw a movement at the corner of his cage and heard a strange rumbling noise. It sounded like his electric toothbrush when its battery was running low. To his astonishment he realised it was Sinbad rubbing against the bars — and the surly ship's cat was purring! Sam stuck his hand through the cage to stroke him, too miserable to wonder if he'd lose a finger or two. "At least you're on my side," he told him as he scratched him under the chin.

"Don't go near that traitor!" came a shrill voice. Charlie stormed up to the cage, dropping the sack she was carrying.

"Charlie, please listen," pleaded Sam. "I know the captain's in danger."

She stooped to pick up the cat. "Sinbad's not the only one on your side," she whispered. "I believe that letter wasn't yours, but I can't be seen to be friendly."

Two of the crew came up onto the foredeck to secure some ropes. Charlie immediately rubbed her face against Sinbad's. "You are a very naughty puss to go near Sam Silver!" she told him sternly.

The men laughed, finished their task and went back down to the main deck.

"Quick, Sam," hissed Charlie. "Tell me what you know."

Sam told her about Dick's signalling. "I'm sure the captain's heading for a trap," he finished.

"Then we'll have to go after him!" declared Charlie. "He needs to be warned. We'll take the other rowing boat."

"Good thinking," said Sam. "He might believe *you*. But there's one little problem. How are you going to tow me along in my cage?"

Charlie pinned Sinbad under one

arm and delved into her pocket, pulling
out a small object that glinted in the
lantern light. "You won't need towing. I
'borrowed' this key from Harry's belt."

"Brilliant!" breathed Sam. He sniffed the
air. "But what's that awful smell? It's worse
than my prison."

"Just a fish head I've got in my pocket,"
said Charlie, airily. "I'll give it to Sinbad to
keep him busy while we go ashore. I don't
want him following us." She produced the
fish head and threw it to the deck. The cat
sprang out of her arms and onto it with a
delighted miaow.

Charlie turned the key in the padlock. It opened with a loud click. She paused, eyes darting over the deck in case someone had heard. Then she swung open the little door and Sam crawled out, stretching painfully and shaking tomato pips out of his hair. Charlie delved into the sack she'd dropped and produced a coconut. She arranged the sack in a pile on the floor of the cage and plonked the coconut next to it. "That looks enough like you to fool the crew for a little while," she whispered. "If anyone goes by they'll think you're asleep."

They crept to the steps that led down to the main deck. Harry Hopp and Ned were patrolling up and down, talking in low voices.

"Now!" hissed Charlie as the two men turned towards the stern. Sam and Charlie made a dash for the side rail. They slid silently over it and were halfway down the footholds to the rowing boat below when

Sam's foot suddenly slipped with a loud *bang!*

"What was that?" came a voice from the deck.

They flattened themselves to the side of the ship. Sam's heart was beating wildly. Were they about to get caught?

CHAPTER TEN

S am and Charlie clung to the ship, not daring to move a muscle.

"Sounded like it came from below," they heard Ned call.

"But something's moving on the foredeck!" said Harry Hopp.

Footsteps crossed above their heads.

"It's only Sinbad up here," came Ned's voice. "He's chasing a fish head.

I don't dare tell him it's already dead!"

A spyglass opened with a snap. "The captain and Dick have almost reached land now," reported Harry. "I can just see the boat."

"As soon as we get word from the captain, we'll be aboard the *Queen Bess.*" Ned chuckled. "I do hope Her Royal Majesty doesn't mind us dipping our fingers into her gold."

"She won't have a choice," laughed Harry. "And there'll be one less to share the booty with." Sam winced as he heard the sound of his cage being kicked. Would they discover that he wasn't inside? He held his breath. No, it was all right, the sack and coconut must be doing their job!

Harry was still talking. "Silver should get all the sleep he can before Captain Blade gets back and throws him off the ship!"

The voices moved away.

Sam and Charlie lowered themselves into the rowing boat. Sam untied the rope from the mooring ring on the hull and pushed off. Charlie kept her eyes firmly on the beach as he rowed swiftly for shore.

"The captain and Dick are still there," Charlie told Sam. "They've got a lantern. I think they're making sure their boat is well hidden."

"We'd better land a bit further along," said Sam, reversing the stroke of his left oar to change their course. "Then we'll stay out of sight until I can distract Dick and you can speak to the captain."

"Agreed," said Charlie. "And we'd better do it before Dick's accomplices get here."

As soon as the water was shallow enough, they leapt out and pulled the boat up the sand.

"We'll use those trees for cover," said Sam, pointing to a dense grove of palms growing along the shore.

They hid among the tall trunks of the palm trees. The silence was broken now and again by the night calls of animals deep in the undergrowth.

"Get down!" whispered Charlie suddenly. "I saw a light."

She and Sam dived into a thicket as a bobbing lantern came into view.

They heard a deep voice. "Are you certain this is the route? There was a much clearer path back there."

"It's Captain Blade!" hissed Charlie.

"And I can see Dick behind him."

The two men came into view. They were a good ship's length away, walking across a clearing in the trees. Dick was carrying a lantern that cast a faint beam onto the tree trunks around. Sam and Charlie shrank back.

"But this way's quicker," Dick answered. "It goes directly to Bridgetown port."

At that moment Sam saw him spread out his free hand.

"What's he doing?" he whispered in Charlie's ear. "Do you think that's another signal?"

"No," replied Charlie, puzzled. "It looks like he's scattering something — but what?"

There was a loud squawking from among the palm leaves and parrots suddenly swooped out of the trees, flying round Dick and the captain in a swirling flock.

"It must be seed!" breathed Sam.

The captain was frozen to the spot as the flapping birds surrounded him. More and more parrots had appeared from the dark, filling the air in a whirlwind of feathers, then swooping down to fight for their share of the feast.

Dick Gudgeon gave a harsh laugh. From behind his back, he slipped his wooden fid out of his belt and raised it.

Sam went to shout a warning but he was too late. Dick brought it down on the back of the captain's head. Blade fell to his knees, swaying groggily.

Sam started forwards but Charlie grabbed his arm.

"We must help him," Sam said angrily, trying to shake her off.

"I agree," said Charlie in his ear. "But not yet. We must get close enough to take Dick by surprise."

Sam knew she was right. They crept

towards the clearing, using the bushes as cover.

"What a piece of luck." Dick was goading Blade as the captain tried to stand up. He lifted his foot and pushed him over. "When I found out you were scared of parrots, it gave me an idea of how to capture you."

"I should have listened to Sam Silver," muttered the captain. Dick kicked him hard in the ribs and Blade fell to the ground. "You're a slimy sea worm," he groaned.

"There's no treasure and no *Queen Bess* either," Dick went on. "There's just a nice big price on your head and I'm going to collect the reward."

Sam and Charlie were close now. Dick hadn't heard them coming. He was too busy gloating. Charlie looked at Sam and motioned with a nod for them to charge. Sam nodded back, then stopped in horror.

Dick Gudgeon had drawn a pistol. He was aiming it at Captain Blade's forehead, his finger on the trigger.

CHAPTER ELEVEN

Sam looked around desperately for a weapon of some kind. He had to stop Dick Gudgeon from shooting Captain Blade.

Just as Sam had decided he would have to rush Dick and knock the pistol away, Dick let out a cruel laugh and swung the barrel of his pistol upwards. He squeezed the trigger, firing a single bullet into the air.

"Just giving my signal," he said. "Now the soldiers will know exactly where to find us. That's why I took us on this path. It's not really quicker. I had to give them time to get here from Bridgetown." He pulled out a length of rope and tied the captain's arms behind his back. "And I'll get a bigger reward if I hand you over alive."

"You're nothing but a lily-livered coward!" gasped Blade. "To think that I trusted you."

Sam tried to get his brain to work. If soldiers were coming he and Charlie needed to rescue the captain now. He felt about the ground and found a stick.

"We must wait," Charlie whispered. "We can't risk Dick shooting the captain."

"I seem to have the sort of face that men trust," Dick told Blade pleasantly, as if they were having a friendly conversation. "You're the third pirate captain I've delivered to Governor Granville. And a very nice pile of gold I've made for myself. Of course, the reward for the great Captain Blade will be double the rest put together."

"By Jupiter, you'll regret this," snarled the captain, struggling against his ropes.

Dick aimed his pistol and shot twice, sending up two spurts of dust near the captain's feet. Blade stopped struggling.

"I'll hand you over dead if I have to," said Dick in his oily voice. "Now, where was I? Oh, yes, then I've got your stronghold to plunder. I remember enough of the map that boy was kind enough to draw for me. He was very useful. First the parrot information and then that."

Sam's blood boiled. He leapt to his feet. But Charlie threw herself at him and pulled him down again. Sam realised she was right. If he made a move, Dick would shoot the captain before they could get anywhere near.

Gudgeon didn't seem to have heard anything. "I won't be telling the governor about that. It's all for me. I'll buy myself a big house on Jamaica and live a life of luxury."

"You'll be for ever looking over your shoulder," snarled the captain, struggling against his bonds. "My men will hunt you down."

"Hunt down the brave Dick Gudgeon who nearly died trying to save you?" laughed the villain. "Surely not. They'll be so grateful, they'll make me captain."

He turned his head at the sound of feet pounding towards them. A second later, a group of armed soldiers burst into the clearing. Quick as a flash, Dick pulled the letter of safe passage from the captain's coat and showed it to their leader.

"I think you'll find this is in order," he said. "And here is your prisoner."

He pointed at his captive and, before Sam and Charlie's horrified eyes, Captain Blade was seized. His bonds were cut, his hands forced out in front of him and iron manacles slapped around his wrists.

The soldiers dragged him away. Dick Gudgeon sauntered along behind, swinging his arms and whistling *Greensleeves*.

The soldiers were taking a rough dirt
track that led along the shoreline. Sam and
Charlie followed, darting from tree to tree,
keeping a safe distance.

"It'll be sunrise soon," Charlie told Sam,
pulling him over to the side of the path.
"We must be careful we're not seen."

"I wonder what's happening on the
Sea Wolf," said Sam. "They must have
noticed that I'm missing. They'll think I've
gone to betray the captain." He gulped,
remembering how awful it was to have the
crew hating him.

"The captain will put them right," said Charlie, squeezing his arm, "when we've rescued him and got him back to the ship."

They walked on as the sun began to appear over the low hills to their left. Here and there, a house lay off the track, and soon there were more, lying closer together.

"We must be coming to Bridgetown," whispered Sam.

The dirt track joined a cobbled street. It was early, but people were already up and about carrying milk churns and baskets of bread. Stalls were being set up for a market. The soldiers pushed their way through the townsfolk, who gawped when they saw the captured pirate and hurled insults at him. Sam could see that, despite his manacled hands and the blow to his head, Blade was walking tall, ignoring the jibes and catcalls of the Bridgetown people.

As they followed the soldiers round a corner they found themselves in a central square. On the other side was a tall, stark building with grey stone walls.

"That's the fort," said Charlie. "That's where they'll take Captain Blade. We can't follow him in there."

Two big gates swung open to let in the soldiers and their prisoner. Dick Gudgeon followed. Sam got a glimpse of crowds of uniformed men inside before the gates were pulled shut.

There was a sudden noise of sliding bolts and a door, barely big enough for a man to pass through, opened in one of the huge gates. Two soldiers emerged.

"That Blade's not so scary when you see him in irons," one was saying.

"And we'll be giving *him* something to be scared of later this morning!" laughed the other. He hammered a large notice to the gate. Then he spotted Sam and Charlie. "Have a look at this," he told them. "Not long to wait for a bit of entertainment!"

As soon as the two men had disappeared back inside the fort, Charlie slipped forwards and read the notice. She turned to Sam, her eyes huge and dark in her pale face.

"What does it say?" he asked.

"It says that Captain Thomas Blade . . ." Charlie gulped. ". . . it says that he'll hang at nine o'clock!"

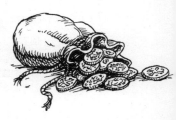

CHAPTER TWELVE

"There's no time to get help from the crew," declared Sam. He took Charlie by the shoulders. "It's up to us. Somehow we've got to get into that fort and rescue him."

Charlie's forehead creased in concentration. "I've got a better idea. The notice says it's going to be a public hanging in the main square here. We'll free him when he's brought out."

"In full view of all the people and soldiers?" gasped Sam. "Not to mention the governor! How will we manage that?"

Charlie gave him a sudden grin. "Trust me!" she said. "Wait here!" The next second she'd vanished into the crowd.

Sam was bewildered. Where was his friend going? As he stood gazing at the heavy arched gates of the fort, he heard a familiar voice behind him.

"Found you at last!"

"Fernando!" exclaimed Sam. He spun round in delight. "Am I glad to see—" He stopped dead. Fernando's teeth were bared in an angry snarl and the blade of his knife flashed in front of Sam's eyes.

"Don't move a muscle!" Fernando pushed him up against the wall and thrust the knife against Sam's throat. "Where are the captain and Dick Gudgeon? You have

betrayed them to the governor, haven't
you? And I expect Charlie is having a nice
cosy chat to Granville right now. Admit it,
before I kill you!"

Sam gulped. "You don't understand,
Fernando. Charlie and I—"

"I understand perfectly!" snapped
Fernando. "As soon as I found that the
two of you had gone, I knew where you'd
be. As you'd used the other boat I swam to
shore to come after you. You're a dirty
traitor, and so is Charlie!"

"It wasn't like that," said Sam
desperately. "*We're* not the traitors. Dick
Gudgeon is." He held his friend's gaze.

"You must believe me. Haven't I always been your friend — and loyal to the *Sea Wolf*?" He quickly told Fernando how they had watched Blade fall into Gudgeon's trap and how the captain was going to be hanged.

For a moment Fernando looked unsure. "I want to believe you, but how can I? The captain is going to be hanged because of you," he said desperately. "You're coming with me. I'm going to tie you up and then rescue him."

The gate to the fort opened again and someone slipped out, whistling. Sam recognised the tune. It was *Greensleeves*. The man strolled away between the stalls, inspecting the food for sale.

"See?" Sam spoke hoarsely. "It's Dick Gudgeon. He's free."

As he spoke, Fernando's eyes grew wide with amazement and then fury. The dagger dropped from Sam's throat.

"Captain Blade's execution is set for nine this morning," said Sam urgently. "Will you help us?"

"You have no need to ask!" declared Fernando, shoving his knife back into his belt. "I should never have doubted you, my friend."

"That's all right," said Sam. "I'm just glad that you believe me now. And listen, I believed Dick was a good 'un when I first met him, too."

"Well, I hope you will forgive me," said Fernando. "Though I'm not sure I can forgive myself."

"Of course I do," said Sam. "We're friends for ever."

Fernando held up his hand. "Let's high five to seal the deal!"

He gave Sam a ringing slap on his palm. Sam sometimes regretted that he'd taught him how to do this — Fernando didn't always know his own strength.

"Now, what's the plan?" Fernando went on.

"I wish I knew," Sam said, rubbing his hand. "Charlie told me to wait here. I'm hoping she's thought of something."

At that moment a small figure pushed through the crowd, carrying a bundle of clothes with a lady's feathered hat wobbling on top. To the boys' surprise it stopped in front of them. Charlie's face popped up between the feathers. She beamed as she saw Fernando.

"I'm so glad you found us!" she exclaimed. "I knew you'd be on our side!"

Fernando gave Sam an embarrassed glance. Sam grinned back. "What's all this for, Charlie?" he asked. "Are we putting on a play?"

"Don't be silly!" exclaimed Charlie, dropping the clothes on the ground. "I borrowed these from a big house down the road. The window was open and no one saw me pop in. I just grabbed what I could."

The boys looked at her, impressed.

"They're going to help us carry out my brilliant plan. We are going to be an elegant young girl attending the hanging with her two servants. An elegant but bad-tempered girl who will have an enormous tantrum just as the captain is brought out. Then, while everyone's looking at *her*, the two servants will whisk Captain Blade away to the *Sea Wolf*! Simple!" She picked out a long silky dress and held it against herself.

"But the soldiers aren't going to let us snatch the captain from under their noses," protested Sam.

"It might work!" said Fernando eagerly. "But we'll need something more to keep the soldiers busy. Sam and I will think of something."

"There's only one problem," Charlie interrupted, looking down at the fine red material. "This dress is too long for me. Fernando, you're tall. You'll have to be the elegant young girl."

Fernando gawped at her.

"Don't stand there looking like a dead fish!" laughed Charlie. She thrust the dress into her friend's arms. "We have to get changed!"

Fernando held the garment at arm's length and stared in disgust at the frills and lace. "I can't wear this!" he spluttered.

"Someone's got to," said Sam, trying to keep his face straight.

"You do it!" Fernando burst out.

"I'm sure Sam would love to help," said Charlie. Sam looked horrified. "But he's too short. You want to help save the captain, don't you, Fernando?"

"Of course I do! But—"

"That's settled then." Charlie passed Sam a blue jacket with brass buttons and a pair of white breeches. "Cheer up, Fernando. We'll be your servants. It'll give you a chance to boss us about. Follow me."

Fernando slunk along behind Charlie, muttering under his breath, as she led them to a quiet alley close to the town square. They hurriedly put on their disguises over their own clothes.

"It's lucky there's enough for three here," said Charlie, pulling on a long braided jerkin. She took her pirate bandana out of her hair and shoved it in her pocket. "Need any help, Fernando?"

Fernando had toppled over, his nose poking out of one of the gown's sleeves and his legs tied up in the folds of the stiff petticoats. Giggling helplessly, Sam and Charlie managed to untangle him and at last he was ready, the hat pulled low, with a feather dangling over his scowling face. Charlie tried to smooth and untangle his long black curls.

"No one will believe that I am a girl," growled Fernando. "Let alone a highborn one."

"They certainly won't if you look like that!" said Charlie. "Stand up straight and try to walk elegantly – and keep your bare feet out of sight. Remember, the captain is depending on you."

Fernando picked up the folds of his skirts and swept off towards the town square. He stopped and swirled round. "Stop dawdling, you good-for-nothing servants!" he called in a high-pitched voice.

"I'll have you whipped if you don't attend me properly."

Grinning, Sam and Charlie scampered after him.

"And I shall require food when I am seated," he went on. "And a drink!"

They came out into the open and stood staring at the scene in front of them. The town square was full of people. Two sides of the square looked out to sea, bounded by low walls with cannon placed at intervals along them. Stalls had been set up to sell beer, fruit and pastries and smoke rose from an ox roasting over an open fire. Chairs stood in rows, all facing a high platform with steps leading up to it. Well-dressed ladies and gentlemen sat eating and chatting cheerfully to each other. The people of Bridgetown were buzzing with the news that a famous pirate captain was soon to be hanged.

In the very centre of the platform stood a wooden framework, with a rope noose swinging in the breeze. It was the gallows. Sam shivered. It was ready for Captain Blade.

Chapter Thirteen

"Come on," muttered Fernando. He began to stride across the square and nearly tripped on his dress. With little mincing steps he approached the two sentries who stood by the gallows. Sam and Charlie hurried after him.

"You there!" Fernando called in his high girly voice. "I am Doña Francesca

Catolina Maria Montoya, daughter of the Spanish Ambassador, and I demand the best seat to watch this pirate hang."

The guards looked at each other, not bothering to keep the smiles from their faces.

Fernando stamped his foot. "I do not like to be kept waiting!" he screeched. "My father will be very angry if he hears that you have not shown me proper respect. He will tell the governor. And the governor does not like his wealthy friends to be upset."

The men looked nervous now and they glanced over at the seats where the well-dressed people were. Sam followed their gaze. He didn't need to be told which of the fine gentlemen was Sir Bevil Granville. A man sat in the middle seat, one hand on the ivory handle of a carved cane. He wore a fine coat and

waistcoat with gold buttonholes all the
way down the front and a massive, curly
brown wig on his head. In the seat next to
the governor sat Dick Gudgeon, wearing a
new hat and smart clothes. He had a smug
look on his face as he waited to see
Captain Blade hang. Sam quickly turned
his head away.

"My father is very important!" snapped
Fernando, his voice getting even shriller.

Some of the gentry started to look round.

"Find her a seat before she gets us into trouble," muttered one of the guards.

They bustled Fernando to the end of the line of chairs. Sam watched Dick out of the corner of his eye, but he was busy fawning over the governor.

Fernando made a great fuss of sorting out his petticoats as he sat down. Then he turned to Sam and Charlie. "Be off with you!" he said imperiously. "Go and sit with the common people!"

Sam and Charlie scampered away.

"It must be nearly nine," said Charlie. "We've got to hurry."

They mingled with the townsfolk round the stalls. The smell of the roasting ox reached his nostrils and Sam's stomach rumbled.

Charlie pointed to a horse and cart, tethered by the fort gate. "That's to take the body away," she gulped.

"No one's guarding it," said Sam. "I think we've found our getaway vehicle."

"What do you mean?" demanded Charlie. "What funny future thing is a 'getaway vehicle'?"

"We'll use it to 'get away' from here," Sam explained, "to make our escape. You know how to drive a cart, don't you?"

Charlie nodded. "Now, Fernando said we'd need to make a diversion after he's had his tantrum. Something that will send the soldiers running away from the captain."

Sam checked out the area. A pile of cannonballs and a keg of powder stood close to one of the cannon, guarded by two men. "You distract those two guards over there," he told Charlie, "and I'll grab some of the gunpowder. A bit of that thrown on the fire should make everyone sit up and take notice!"

Charlie ran towards the guards, holding her hands up to her face. "Help me," she wailed. "A thief just stole my penny and my mistress will beat me when I don't return with her ribbons, and I can't buy the ribbons because the thief stole my penny and my mistress will beat me." She broke into sobs, pulling at the men's jackets.

Sam took his chance. He slipped over to the keg behind them. The lid was loosely on. Keeping an eye on the men, he pushed it aside and scooped out a handful of powder. Then he slunk away.

Charlie felt in the pocket of her borrowed jerkin. "Oh!" she gasped. "Silly me. Here's my penny!" And she ran to join him, leaving the guards scratching their heads.

The church clock began to toll nine and a slow drumbeat could be heard from inside the fort. The large gates opened and a squad of soldiers marched out. The crowd gave a great cheer as they saw Captain Blade in the middle, chained and manacled. He turned and gave them all a defiant bow. The guards led him up the steps to the gallows.

Sir Bevil Granville stood and held out a scroll.

"As Her Majesty Queen Anne's representative in this fair island, I declare that this is Thomas Blade, known pirate, and he shall hang by the neck until he is dead."

The crowd cheered again, led by Dick Gudgeon. A man wearing a black mask

stepped up on to the platform and pushed the captain towards the noose. A priest came forwards and the crowd quietened as he began to murmur prayers.

"This is not to be borne!" A tremendous shriek filled the air and Fernando jumped to his feet. "I cannot see anything from here!"

The people nearest to him put their fingers to their lips but Fernando screamed again. Some of the sentries came over to him, trying to make him sit down. Fernando kicked out at his chair, sending it flying with a crash. "You expect me to sit on that as if I were a common kitchen maid. My father is Don Cristiano Montoya and he will have you all flogged!"

Fernando pushed the woman who'd been sitting next to him. She fell against her neighbour and the whole row toppled like dominos.

Sam could see that Blade had a smile
on his lips. His heart leapt. The captain
had recognised Fernando. He knew there
was a rescue plot afoot. Now it was time
for him and Charlie to carry out their
part. There were still some guards around
the captain and they had to draw them
away.

With one hand, Sam whipped the
kerchief from his neck and spread the
cloth out. He tipped the gunpowder into
the middle and swiftly tied the corners
together.

While the crowd gawped at Fernando's
tantrum, Sam lobbed the package at the

roasting ox. It hit it on the nose and vanished into the flames. A second passed and then . . . *BOOM!*

Chapter Fourteen

Clouds of black smoke filled the
square and lumps of sizzling beef
rained down on the terrified spectators.

"Blackheart's attacking!" Sam shouted at
the top of his voice.

"You get the captain, I'll get the cart!"
Charlie yelled in his ear. A second later
she'd disappeared into the crowd.

Women screamed, soldiers ran to

man the cannon, and dogs and urchins fought for the pieces of falling meat. Eyes stinging from the smoke, Sam wove through the panicking townspeople towards the gallows. Only one guard stood next to the captain, fist firmly clamped round his chains. There was no sign of Fernando anywhere. Sam hoped he was all right but he had no time to look for him now. He had to focus on the captain.

He crept up the steps behind the soldier and poked him hard in the back. The soldier swung round and Sam put his thumbs in his ears, waggled his fingers and stuck his tongue out at him.

"Oi, you little varmint!" growled the guard, dropping his hold on Blade's chains. He advanced on Sam, his hand raised ready to strike him. Captain Blade immediately whacked him on the head with his heavy manacles. As the man tottered towards the edge of the platform, Sam promptly stuck out a foot and tipped him off into the crowd.

"By Satan, you're a sight for sore eyes!" exclaimed Blade. "Now it's time to run!"

"We can go a lot faster than that," said Sam. "Look!"

The crowd was parting in fresh panic as a horse and cart charged at top speed into the square.

Charlie was perched on the front, clutching the reins. "Out of the way!" she shrieked. "Runaway horse!" The cart swerved round the stalls, knocking apples, oranges and pastries all over the place and scattering the onlookers who ran in terror.

"Get ready to jump!" cried Sam.

As the horse thundered past the gallows,
Sam and the captain sprang from the
platform and landed with a thud in the
back of the cart.

The wild-eyed horse reared up with a
loud neigh at the sound and clattered off
down a cobbled street. The cart jolted
along behind.

Sam looked over his shoulder. A band
of soldiers was running after them,
shouting and firing as they made their

escape. The horse galloped round a corner, sending the cart onto two wheels. For a moment Sam thought it would overturn. Then it righted itself and they were heading out of town. There was no sign of the soldiers now.

"That was brilliant, Charlie!" called Sam. "Everyone believed the horse was out of control!"

"It was!" shrieked Charlie, as they rattled along at top speed. "I can't stop it!"

Sam gripped the side of the cart. Had they saved the captain just to kill him in a road accident? Then he saw Charlie give a huge wink.

"I'm joking," she said, pulling on the reins. The horse began to slow to a canter. "I'm in charge — not Dobbin." The cart hit a rut and she was nearly thrown from the driver's seat.

"But not in charge of the road!" laughed Sam.

Then he remembered Fernando. Where was their friend? Was he safe? He tried not to worry. Fernando was wily and brave. He'd be OK.

"Sam Silver," said Captain Blade. He was looking at him intently, his manacled hands held out in front of him for balance. "I am truly sorry for believing that scoundrel and not you," he went on. "I let appearances blind me."

"Don't worry about it," said Sam, a bit embarrassed. "Dick seemed a great bloke and he was very clever. He knew how to say the right things."

"Well, I swear on the *Sea Wolf* that I will never doubt you again, no matter how strange things turn." The captain's face suddenly broke into a broad grin. "And talking of strange things, just wait until I tell Harry how you all turned up to rescue me with Fernando in a dress . . . Where is he?"

"We couldn't find him in all the rush," said Charlie anxiously.

"Then we must go back this instant!" demanded Blade.

"No, Captain, sir," Charlie replied without turning round. "I'm in control of this horse and we're not stopping until we reach our rowing boat."

"And then we're not stopping until you're safe on board," finished Sam. "You're a marked man. We'll come back for Fernando afterwards."

A loud cheer went up as the *Sea Wolf* crew caught sight of Captain Blade being rowed towards the ship. Sam moored the boat to the hull and Harry Hopp spotted the captain's chains.

"What has that villain Silver done?" he called down fiercely.

"He and Charlie have saved my life," the captain called back. "With a little help from Fernando. Sam Silver was right all along. It was Dick Gudgeon who was the villain."

He was helped on board and as Ned went off to fetch an axe to break the chains, the captain told the crew about the trap that had been set for him and how Sam, Charlie and Fernando had saved him.

Shuffling their feet and red in the face, the men of the *Sea Wolf* came one by one to apologise to Sam. He listened with half an ear. He was worrying about Fernando. Had he been hurt in the explosion? Or had Dick Gudgeon found him?

"Boat ahoy!" came a cry.

Sam rushed to the rail with the others. Had the governor sent soldiers after them? No, it was the *Sea Wolf*'s other rowing boat and the rower looked familiar. There was a heaped tarpaulin at the back of the boat.

"Sink me!" exclaimed Harry Hopp, stamping the end of his wooden leg on the deck. "That's Dick Gudgeon. I reckon he's done harm to Fernando. Where's me pistol?"

CHAPTER FIFTEEN

"Hold hard, Harry," declared the captain. "I'll not have a man shot in the back. Let him on board. Perhaps he doesn't know of my escape and is still pretending to be loyal to the *Sea Wolf*. He may have news of the young lad."

Sam watched as the tarpaulin began to wriggle and writhe. Then a grinning face popped out.

"It's Fernando!" Sam yelled in jubilation.

"And he's got Dick's own pistol trained on him," gasped Charlie. "He's taken the scoundrel prisoner!"

"No wonder Dick's rowing so well," said Ned cheerfully.

His face white with fear, Dick Gudgeon scrambled up onto the deck with Fernando close behind, still wearing the dress. At once Dick was seized in the strong grip of Ned and Harry Hopp.

"Captain Blade," he whimpered. "I'm so glad you're all right. I think there has been a misunderstanding." He suddenly set eyes on Sam. "What is that villain doing here? He will be your downfall, Captain, mark my words."

"Belay your cowardly talk or by Mars I'll run you through," thundered the captain. "He's brought about *your* downfall and I owe my life to him and his friends."

Sam and Charlie rushed over to Fernando.

"We were really worried about you," said Charlie. "What happened?"

"I got Dick to bring me here," said Fernando, airily smoothing down his petticoats. "It was the least he could do after all the trouble he's caused."

Sam saw the mischievous glint in his friend's eyes. "And how did you do that?"

"I'm glad you asked, my friend," said Fernando. "I saw him in the smoke and confusion. I believe he was trying to sneak off. So I ran up to him and put on my best girly voice . . ." Fernando carried on in a high-pitched whine. "Help me. I am Doña Francesca Catolina Maria Montoya and my father will pay you handsomely if you rescue me from the invasion."

Dick muttered angrily under his breath. "He was totally fooled by his own greed,"

Fernando told them. "But as soon as he had led me away from the square, I shoved my hat in his face and used the sash from that stupid dress to tie him up. Then I stole a mule and rode to the beach to see if I could find one of the *Sea Wolf* rowing boats. Dick had to lie over the beast's back and I'm sure he had a nice bumpy ride."

"It's no more than he deserves," growled Harry Hopp.

"But why were you under the tarpaulin?" asked the captain. "We could have turned the cannon on the boat when we saw this villain was rowing."

"We heard soldiers coming," said Fernando, "so I decided to hide and let this snivelling sea snail do all the work. He was happy to do so when I threatened him with his own gun." He untied a bag that was fastened to his belt. It was bulging with coins. "And I suggested that he might like to give us the reward money the governor gave him for capturing Captain Blade!"

"Excellent!" exclaimed Blade, slapping Fernando on the back. "The reward for my capture and death. It seems fitting that we should have it. But we mustn't tarry in these waters any longer. Let's dispose of Mr Gudgeon and be on our way. Fetch the plank, Ben!"

As the plank was fixed over the side of the ship, the captain turned to Dick. "You'll make it to shore, I've no doubt," he said, "but you may not want to linger there. The governor will believe that you're one of us. After all, how else did I escape after you'd been paid?"

Ben shoved Dick up onto the plank. The man turned and stared at them angrily. "Aye, I'll make it to shore," he spat. "And then, when you least expect it, I'll sail to your hideout and take everything you've got. You haven't enough men to keep it guarded for ever." He walked to the end of the plank and stared down at the water.

Harry Hopp stomped up on the plank to stop him, but with a triumphant laugh, Dick jumped. The crew looked accusingly at Sam.

"Don't worry," Sam said with a grin. "I'm not that stupid. I put a false location on the map. Dick will find himself heading for the Cloud of Death."

The crew cheered at the thought of Gudgeon finding himself lost in the thick bank of fog that sailors spoke of with terror.

"There's a fin following him," cried Charlie, pointing out towards the shore.

"It's probably just a dolphin," said Captain Blade. Sam could hear a tinge of disappointment in his voice.

"But hopefully it's a shark!" muttered Fernando. "One of his own kind."

"Aye to that!" declared Ned. The crew cheered again.

"Blast the blackguard!" squawked Crow, peering down at them from the top of the mast.

Captain Blade glanced up, then wiped

his forehead nervously as he strode over to take the wheel.

"Weigh anchor!" shouted Harry Hopp, and at once the deck was a bustle of activity. Sam realised that any minute now the coin would whisk him back to the future.

"I may need to check on my mum soon," he told the captain. "I don't want to leave, but I have to go to the supermarket for some milk . . ."

The captain stared at him.

"Supermarket is the name of his cow," said Charlie quickly. "Sam's got to go and milk her."

Captain Blade slapped him on the back. "Just make sure you hurry back, young Silver. This crew needs you."

"Aye, aye Captain!" said Sam, a huge smile on his face. He turned to Charlie. "Thank you for believing in me. You're a true friend."

Charlie's cheeks went pink.

Sinbad slunk out from behind a barrel and stared at him, unblinking.

Sam knelt down. "And thank *you* for being friendly when I was locked in that cage," he said, holding out a hand to pet the cat.

Merow! Just in time, Sam snatched his hand out of the way of a vicious swipe.

He grinned happily at Charlie. "If Sinbad's back to normal then everything's back to normal!"

Sam suddenly felt his fingers and toes begin to tingle. The coin was about to take him home. He dived out of sight and into the storeroom as he felt himself sucked up into the dark, whirling tunnel that would carry him through time.

A moment later, Sam landed on his bedroom carpet. He jumped up and put

the coin safely away in its bottle. Now
he had to run to the supermarket for his
mum. He was glad he didn't have to try
and milk a cow! He had to admit that lots
of things were much easier in his modern
world – but not half as exciting as life on
the *Sea Wolf*!

The Sea Wolf

Charlie Fleetwood
Deckhand

Ben Hudson
Quartermaster

Sam Silver
Lookout

Ned Wainwright
Bosun

Harry Hopp
First Mate

CREW MANIFEST

Sinbad

Crow

Thomas Blade
Captain

Peter Craddock
Ship's Cook

Fernando
Rigger

Don't miss the next exciting adventure in the
Sam Silver: Undercover Pirate series

DRAGON FIRE

Available in February 2013!
Read on for a special preview
of the first chapter.

CHAPTER ONE

Sam Silver opened his eyes and
jumped out of bed. It was Saturday
and Saturday meant a fantastic game
of football down on the beach with his
mates. But he could hear a spattering
sound against his bedroom window. He
pulled the curtains and groaned – rain
was coming down in sheets! The high
street was deserted and he could hardly

see the sand of Backwater Bay in the grey
mist. His heart sank to the bottom of
his pyjamas. There'd be no football this
morning.

He glanced over at the shelf on his
bedroom wall. It was covered in things he'd
found washed up by the sea. In the middle
stood the old sand-pitted bottle that was
more valuable to him than the World Cup!

Inside lay a gold doubloon, put there three hundred years ago by his pirate ancestor, Joseph Silver. The coin had the power to take him back in time to the *Sea Wolf*, a real pirate ship.

"Well, if I can't play footie," he said to the bottle, "I'll have an adventure instead – in the hot Caribbean sunshine."

Sam knew no one would miss him. No time ever passed in the present when he was back in 1706. He quickly dressed in the scruffy jeans and T-shirt that he always wore when he took up his buccaneer duties. He tipped the coin out of the bottle, spat on it and rubbed it on his sleeve.

Sam's bedroom walls began to spin. He caught a glimpse of his rain-soaked window rushing by before he was lifted into the dark tunnel of time and whooshed around. It was like being inside a monster vacuum cleaner. The next instant he found himself sitting on the floor of the storeroom of the *Sea Wolf*. But the ship was tipping violently from side to side. He was flung against a barrel then thrown onto a coil of rope. The ship's timbers creaked and groaned as if they were going to break.

"Batten down the hatches!" came a squawk and the ship's parrot, flew out from behind a chest and landed on his shoulder.

"Hello there, Crow," said Sam, delighted to see his feathery friend. "What's happening? Let's get up on deck and see."

He spotted his belt, spyglass and jerkin scattered across the floor. His friend Charlie had left them for him, as she always did when Sam was whisked home to the future. The bold girl pirate was the only one on board who knew his time-travelling secret. He was pleased to see that she'd found him a new neckerchief too — he'd blown the last one up. Sam put on his pirate gear and grabbed hold of the door handle. The tossing motion of the ship flung him against the door, but with the next roll, he forced it open and burst out. He staggered up the steps to the main deck.

There was no sign of the sparkling sea and blue Caribbean sky that he usually saw when he arrived in the past. Fierce black clouds raced overhead and waves crashed against the sides of the ship. Rain hammered the deck, drenching him instantly. Through the downpour he could see the captain struggling to keep the wheel steady.

Harry Hopp, a stocky pirate with a wooden leg, was hauling on a rope. "Someone help me get these sails round," he yelled.

With Crow clinging to his shoulder, Sam lurched across the streaming deck. He joined the first mate and seized the end of the rope.

"I'll help you, Mr Hopp," he bellowed over the wind, pulling with all his strength.

"Stap me!" cried Harry, his stubbly face breaking into a broad grin. "It's Sam Silver! How did you get here in this storm?"

Sam didn't know what to say. "Er . . . I . . . well . . ." he spluttered. Charlie usually got him out of this sort of pickle, but she was nowhere to be seen. Then it came to him. "I got here before the storm started!"

"I never saw you," shouted Harry.

"Never saw you," the parrot repeated helpfully.

"Of course not," panted Sam as he worked. "That's because, er . . . I was just coming up on deck when the storm began. Yes, that's it, and I got thrown about and bumped my head and . . ."

Two huge hands took hold of the rope behind him.

"Well, boil me up for breakfast!" It was

Ned the cheerful bosun. "The poor boy must have knocked himself out! And yet here he is, getting to work straight away."

"Aye," said Harry, lashing the rope to a strong wooden hook. "He's a true Silver, just like his grandfather, God rest his soul."

The pirates thought that Sam was Joseph Silver's grandson. Sam went along with this. He couldn't tell them just how many "greats" there really were in between.

"We're glad you're back!" called Captain Blade from the wheel. The weapons in the belts across his chest glistened with rain, and his dark hair and beard hung in rats' tails.

Sam battled through the wind to reach him.

"Keep your distance," ordered the captain, eyeing Crow who was still on Sam's shoulder. Captain Blade was the bravest man Sam knew, but the sight of the green bird always made him go pale. Peter the cook claimed it was because a parrot had pooed on him in his pram, but every pirate on the *Sea Wolf* had a different story about the reason for the captain's one fear. However, they all agreed about one thing – when Captain Blade was around, the parrot was to be called a Caribbean crow. That way the captain could pretend he had nothing to be scared of.

Blade looked up at the sky. "By Orion, I think the storm's abating ahead," he said. "Those clouds don't look as heavy and I'd bet a bag of doubloons that the waves aren't as high."

"We'll soon be back on course," agreed Harry Hopp.

"Where were you heading?" asked Sam.

"Till this weather came along, we were

following a French treasure fleet," the captain told him.

"They'll be scattered in the storm by now," said Harry Hopp with a cunning grin. "Easier to make one of them a target."

Great! thought Sam. *A treasure hunt.*

"Set sail north-east," ordered the captain. "There's nothing can stop us now."

Someone came pounding up the steps from the gun deck below. One look at the long curly hair and bright bandana and Sam knew it was his friend Fernando.

He ran across to greet him, but Fernando was making straight for Captain Blade. He was muttering under his breath in Spanish.

"We're leaking, Captain!" he cried. "And it's bad!"

Find out how the adventures began in . . .

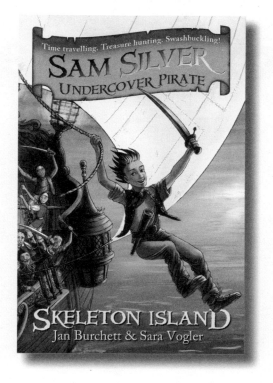

Join Sam Silver aboard the pirate ship,
Sea Wolf, for a rip-roaring adventure
on the high seas! Can Sam lead the crew
to buried treasure, or will he be forced
to walk the plank?

the
orion star

Sign up for **the orion star**
newsletter to get inside information
about your favourite children's authors
as well as exclusive competitions and
early reading copy giveaways.

www.orionbooks.co.uk/newsletters

Follow on

Orion
Children's Books